JINGU

The Hidden Princess

by Ralph Pray
Illustrations by Xiaojun Li

Shen's Books
an imprint of Lee & Low Books
New York

To my grandchildren, Kelly and Henry
—R. E. Pray

Shen's Books, an imprint of LEE & LOW BOOKS INC.,
95 Madison Avenue, New York, NY 10016
leeandlow.com

Book design by Andrea Miles and NeuStudio
Book production by The Kids at Our House
The display text was set in Calligraphic 421
The body text was set in Leawood

Manufactured in the United States of America
by Worzalla Publishing Company
10 9 8 7 6 5 4 3 2
First Lee & Low Paperback Edition
Paperback ISBN 978-1-885008-98-5

Library of Congress Cataloging-in-Publication Data

Pray, Ralph E.
The hidden princess / by Ralph E. Pray ; illustrations by Xiaojun Li.
p. cm.
Summary: In fourth-century Japan, a princess lives a life of loneliness and
learning until she makes a secret friend, but her destiny forbids that they
ever be more than friends.
ISBN 1-885008-21-X
[1. Kings, queens, rulers, etc.—Fiction. 2. Friendship—Fiction. 3. Family life—
Japan—Fiction. 4. Japan—History—To 645—Fiction.] I. Li, Xiaojun, ill. II. Title.
PZ7.P897 Hi 2001
[Fic]—dc21
2002000290

MIX
Paper from
responsible sources
FSC   FSC® C002589
www.fsc.org

My Birthday

I am not allowed visitors, although servants come and go.

I am Princess Jingu, the great grandchild of Keko, twelfth Imperial Emperor of Japan. It is said he was a Great Ruler with forty wives. What I remember best about him is the number of his children — eighty. That must be why there now are so many princes and princesses.

Today is my tenth birthday in this year of A.D. 347. But there is to be no party. My mother hides me from everyone except my teachers and Badiko, my governess. My parents live in the Palace house connected to my house. Badiko and I live in four rooms with two doors. One door goes into the palace and has two Imperial Guards who stand in the corridor.

4   My Birthday

They have swords and spears. I often listen through the wall to the guards when they talk. The only door to the outside world I can use leads to an open courtyard with high walls. I run barefoot outside to play alone before morning tea.

My white cat, Skoki, will not go out with me unless I carry her out. She has a mind of her own, but is very polite about doing things her way.

Old Chu Soy from China is my teacher. I learn writing from him. He gives each Japanese word a Chinese symbol. We speak Japanese but there is no written Japanese language.

The palace is a low cluster of many buildings made of stone, wood, and clay brick. These hundreds of meeting rooms and homes are connected by pebble and dirt paths. The roofs are made of thatched straw.

Badiko calls from the doorway, "Come in for your morning tea, Royal Child."

I skip in from the courtyard. "Badiko, please look at me. Are my eyes any smaller today?"

The answer is the same every morning. "You have intelligent eyes, Princess. But they are no smaller today than they were yesterday. They look large only because your young face is so narrow."

"Mother hates my eyes."

"Ah, so. It only seems that way, Royal Child."

But I know. She's kept me hidden ever since I grew like a beanstalk four years ago. I had friends before then. Now she is always worried about what people will say. She protests that I am too tall for my age, and that I am skinny with bumps on my knees and thighs like a bamboo pole. She complains that my eyes are too big. She is very pretty and is ashamed of my strange appearance. I have no friends now, not even one. Skoki is my friend, of course. But cats don't talk. If Skoki could answer me I'd ask her why she sits looking away from me every time I talk to her. I wonder if all cats pretend they're not listening. Mother also sometimes turns away from me when I'm talking to her.

"Tend to your lessons, Princess," Badiko tells me, "and forget your troubles with Lady Katsuraki. Your mother is an important Court lady. She has the attention of many people and is very busy. Only your learning will get you out of your little prison here."

I gulp my tea while Badi fusses with my coal-black hair. She makes a big coil of my tresses and piles it on top of my head. I go back out in the court-yard. I sit on the low stone wall around the fish pond, beside a garden of bushes and flowers. I think about how nice it would be to have a friend. Even better than a white pearl. The servants say that a princess given a white pearl as a token of respect will live a life of happiness.

A round mud-pie lies flat on top of the wall beside me. The mud is still wet and smooth from my patting. It is my birthday cake. I pat it again and scratch the number "10" with a stick on the stiff, brown surface.

"Princess!" Badiko calls from the doorway. "Your father is here. Wash the mud from your hands. Hurry."

I swish my fingers between the lily pads in the pond water until the mud is gone. I dry them on my long white shirt and dash inside. My father, Prince Tarashi, is opening a small basket on Badiko's stone table. He wears a dark blue kimono and brown leather sandals. His hair is bunched up on top of his head and tied tightly with black silk ribbons. It sticks straight up and makes him look tall. There are many princes like my father in the Royal Family, most of whom are officials in the Imperial Court.

"Good morning, Father." I bow three times.

"Jingu, your mother does not want you sitting by the fishpond. You could fall in and drown."

It seems that my parents worry about silly things. "Father, I will never fall in. Even if I did, I would just stand up. The water is not deep."

"You are stubborn. You may be right but don't argue with her. She doesn't like it." He smiles. "See here. I have brought you gifts for your birthday. The Emperor sends you this little mirror of bronze set in a wood frame. I don't believe you have ever seen a mirror before. He asked me to place it in your hands. It is the Court gift for Royal Girls at the age of ten. Your mother and I give you these tea leaves. They come from China, a journey of six months."

"Thank you, Father. I would also like a friend, please."

"Impossible! That can be dangerous. There may be enemies who would act like friends. You must be protected."

"What enemies, Father?"

"People who envy you because of your royal blood and your success at lessons. The high fences and alert guards are here for your security. We also have many family friends in the Court and in the military who are concerned for your well-being. As you grow older you will learn that some people might not like you. It's the same for everyone, perfectly normal. You need not worry about it."

"I'm not worried, Father."

"Good. I hope you like your gifts."

"I do, Father. The mirror is a nice surprise. Will you please thank the Emperor for me."

"Yes, Jingu, I will. It's time for me to go. Your mother is waiting for me."

Father kisses me goodbye.

Am I really being protected? I've asked Chu Soy about that more than once, and his answer is never "yes." I've decided to become a soldier so I can protect myself and others like me. It's my biggest secret.

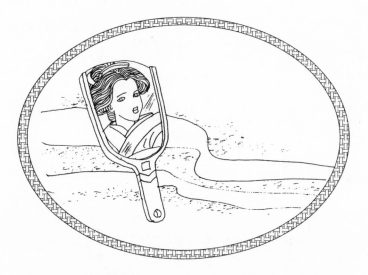

THE MIRROR'S SECRET

I pick up Skoki and the metal mirror and carry them outside. I look at myself by the light of the sun. Oh, I do have big eyes! No one I have ever seen has a face like mine. But I like my eyes. I think they may help me see more of everything around me. I kneel down on the ground beside Skoki and hold the mirror in front of her. She turns away, not interested in seeing herself, or at least pretending not to be. Maybe she has mirrors in her cat's eyes and can see herself anytime she wants to.

Skoki runs in the house with her tail straight up when I walk over to the fish pond with the mirror. I sit on the low wall, where my parents think I'm in danger of falling in the water. The deepest place is just over my knees when I stand up. Goodness, I've

10   The Mirror's Secret

been in the water a hundred times when Badiko isn't looking, trying to catch one of the golden fish. I wonder if they're slippery. All I know is, they're very quick and not interested in my friendship. I hold the mirror up again. It's heavy for such a small thing, and it looks important.

The mirror frame is of thick polished wood. I see the ends of tiny slots in the wood where the mirror must have been slid into it. I wonder what the back of the mirror looks like, if it's shiny like the front. Could I see the back of my head in it? I press my thumbs on the shiny metal and try to slide it out of the slots. It's stuck in there, perhaps with the glue made from fish. I push harder — nothing. I tap the frame on the rock wall to see if the shock will break it loose. I push the metal again with my thumbs. It moves! I keep pushing until the metal part slides out of the slots. I turn it over. Yuck! It's just unpolished metal. But inside the wood is something interesting.

Where the mirror had covered the holder someone has drawn my name in Chinese with black iron ink. I know the ink is forever. Chu Soy says iron ink will last thousands of years. But there is more than just my name. It says, "Imperial Princess Jingu."

I feel the little hairs on the back of my neck tickle with alarm. There is no Imperial Princess in the Royal Family. That is just below being married to the Emperor, one step beneath Empress. The youngest girl marries at thirteen, and I am only ten.

What does the writing mean? Even my mother, who is very powerful in the Court, will never receive that title. Who can I ask about it? Anyone? No! It is a hidden secret and is meant to be kept a secret beneath the mirror. I feel something strong inside me, like I felt when I was very young and my mother hugged me. Some very clever person in the Royal Court must be thinking about me. I slide the mirror back into its slots and go into the house to study with my teachers.

My lessons go all day every day from morning tea to bedtime. I love to learn new things, to write with a brush and black ink on freshly-made paper. I do numbers with wooden beads sliding on slim bamboo rods.

Chu Soy speaks slowly, saying each lesson word as if it's a jewel to be polished. "Everything known in Japan comes from the spoken word, Heavenly Princess. Your history has been handed down through stories and songs for centuries."

"Chu Soy, why is there no Japanese writing for our words?"

"The people work so hard, Heavenly One, they have no time to invent written words. A time will come for Japanese writing, I am sure. Perhaps the storytellers will be the inventors."

I know there are hundreds of priests, princes, soldiers, and servants living in the sprawling buildings near me. I ask him, "Do many storytellers live in the palace?"

"Yes, Royal One. They tell the history of Japan. Only recently has Chinese writing been taught by a few visitors such as your humble servant."

Without hinting to Chu Soy about my secret behind the mirror or my wish to become a soldier, I ask him, "What can a princess become instead of just a Court Lady in a pretty kimono?"

"You, Heavenly Flower, shall be what you wish to be."

I like his answer and think about it a lot. That night, my birthday night, I hear loud talking through one wall of my room. Father must have left the sliding door open on the closet between our houses. I wrap my fur blanket around me and sit on the floor next to the gray paper wall. I listen.

My father speaks. "Yes, I told her not to sit near the pond."

Mother's complaining voice comes to me. "Jingu is such a stubborn child, as if she had a mind of her own. Why? Oh, why was I not given a brave son instead of this skinny daughter?"

I crawl into my fur bedding wishing I was a son. I am as unloved as the mud-pie on the pond wall. I cry silently.

Journey to Mizo

On the day I turn eleven Badiko is called into my parent's home next to mine. She is gone a long time while I study with Chu Soy. I ask him, "Do you know what they're talking about?"

"No, Royal Child. It is not a matter of discipline, I am certain, unless you've done something I don't know about."

"I haven't done anything wrong for a long time. I'm too busy with my lessons to get into trouble. Oh, I found a toy spear someone had thrown over the wall into the courtyard. I practice throwing it when no one is looking, and I hide it in the garden shrubs. I know Mother would take it away from me if she heard about it."

"Secrets that can cause trouble have to be handled carefully, Little Princess. Perhaps your new toy is not really a spear but may be called an exercise rod. Think how to use words to guide the thoughts of your listener."

Everything Chu Soy says is important to me. I close my eyes and remember his words. He uses them to guide my thoughts. The idea of calling my spear something else, words that still fit it, is very big in my mind, like a ripe apple so fat I can't get my fingers all the way around it. My teacher from China, who knows me even better than Badiko, sees me thinking and nods his head with approval.

I hear a noise at the door. It's Badiko talking to the guards. I jump up to greet her. She comes in wearing a big smile. Her face is red with excitement.

"What is it, Badi? What happened?"

"We are going away, Royal Child, on a trip to the shrine at Mizu."

"To the seashore?"

"Yes, Princess. We leave in the morning, just you and me. And, of course, the guards and servants."

"For how long?"

"Ah, so. Just one day, Royal One. Long enough to give thanks at the holy place. We must return before dark."

Away, away. I'm going away. Leaving the palace, if only for a day. A great adventure. Suddenly I feel so light I must be floating. My feet are surely above the floor, dancing in the air like leaves whisked about by the wind. I run to Badiko and hug her. "Thank you, Badi, for bringing such good news."

"Ah, so. Your mother has told me how you are to dress, Princess. We have to get your things ready tonight."

I have a big question. "Badi, Mother has never let me do anything like this before. What happened to make her change her mind?"

Badiko shuffles to the stove in her slippered feet and feeds a piece of charcoal to the red coals. Without looking at me she says, "I'm not sure what happened, Royal Child. Lady Katsuraki may have received instructions concerning you."

I turn to Chu Soy seated at the study table. His wise old eyes glimmer in the light coming through the open courtyard door. "What do you think, Chu Soy?

"The suddenness of the departure, Heavenly One, may indicate someone wishes to put this decision in the past as rapidly as possible."

My teacher and my governess are both telling me my mother may have been told to let me go away on a short trip. I ask Chu Soy, "Who would tell my mother to do that?"

Now Chu Soy turns away from me before speaking, a thing he rarely does. "We shall perhaps learn of this before long, Heavenly Child."

"Will it be safe for me to go to Mizu? My father is always worried about enemies out to get me."

Chu Soy chuckles. "It's natural for a father to fret about his daughter's safety, Little Princess. I'm sure you'll be well guarded on your trip."

The next day at dawn Badiko dresses me in thick rabbit furs and deer-hide footwear. After a breakfast of rice and fish we leave the house through the corridor door. The sky is turning from black to deep blue. We walk on a wide dirt path to a nearby group of sturdy-looking barefoot men dressed in simple breechcloths. My father and the two guards from our door are there. They stand around a litter, a couch for carrying people.

"Good morning, Father." I bow three times.

"Well, Jingu. This is a treat for you. Are you happy?"

"Yes, very happy. Thank you, Father."

"You've done well in your lessons, Daughter. This trip is a reward for those efforts. These two guards will stay with your carriers. There will be other palace guards among the people you see along the way. Soldiers on horseback will be up ahead of you and somewhere behind you. Many people will be watching you, so be a good young lady. You must mind Badiko during your journey."

"I will. Thank you, Father."

"I'll meet you here tonight as you return. Goodbye."

I say goodbye to Father and sit on the couch with Badiko. Four men pick up the carry poles and we bounce away. I have to hold on to keep from sliding off the litter. We're still on the palace grounds. Early risers stand to the side as our group passes by. People look at us with quick glances. Badiko is easy to see, her grey hair covered with a white silk scarf. My rabbit-fur hood covers my whole head except for my nose and eyes. I bounce and sway so much I almost complain to Badiko. But she is on the same couch, and is also holding on to the back. If I hold on extra-tight I don't bounce any more, but then each big step the carriers take makes my head snap. I think I'd rather walk.

Now we're on a road wide enough for riders on horseback to pass each other. The bare feet of the carriers thump on a wooden bridge over a stream. We go around a hill and I see the orange sun on the horizon below. Two palace guards ride over the bridge we just crossed. Their horses' hooves clatter loudly in the morning stillness. I see wet fields ahead. There are women bent over in the shallow water, planting green rice shoots.

Badiko asks, "Are you warm enough, Princess?"

"Yes, Badi. My furs keep the heat inside." I lower my hood and feel the cold air on my ears.

The carriers change walking speed. We go fast. We come to a small village. I see a palace guard on horseback up ahead. The guards all wear leather vests with metal strips hanging from their shoulders. The strips make a clinking sound when the guards walk or move about. I see people walking in both directions on the road. They stop as we approach, and bow deeply. Some of the people lie on the ground on their stomachs, arms outstretched toward us, faces in the dirt. It is called reverence.

"Badi, they shouldn't do that. I'm only a little princess."

"Ah, so. Never mind, Princess Jingu. The people are honored that someone from the Royal Family pays a visit. They are thanking you."

Now there are men and women lying on the ground on both sides. No one but us is moving. It is quiet except for the creaking of the carry poles holding our couch. The bare feet of the carriers and soldiers make no sound. Children also lie on the ground, between the elders, their faces pointed down in the dirt. I wonder if they're afraid. I pretend I'm the Emperor, and these people love me. It gives me a feeling of importance. Just then three chickens, squawking loudly, flutter across the road in front of us. Badiko covers her face to hide her laugh. I pull my hood over my head and try not to giggle.

In the distance I see the blue of the ocean. We leave the hills and enter into the lowlands, where rice fields stretch as far as I can see. A man bent over with his head almost touching the ground stands aside for us. He carries a load on his back twice as big as he.

"Badi, what does that man carry?"

"A load of firewood, Princess."

We pass many walking people who carry things on their backs. I see an old man with four cages, a rooster in each one. There is a woman with two children tightly bound to her back and a baby feeding at her breast. The world away from the palace is so interesting. I can't stop looking for even a blink of my eyes. We arrive at a village along the seashore as the sun reaches its highest place. The carriers set us down and disappear as a welcoming group surrounds us, bowing and smiling. We step down from the couch. The steady ground feels good after the swaying ride. Badiko takes charge, first telling our guards they can go for the mid-day meal.

The mayor of the village comes forward from the crowd with a few words to offer Badiko a gift wrapped in a black silk cloth. Everyone is bowing up and down and smiling as Badi accepts the token.

She turns to me. "This is your gift from the people of the village, Royal Child." She holds the little silk bundle in her upturned open hands.

I undo the knot at the top and spread the ends apart in her palms. There on the shimmering black silk in Badiko's hands are a cluster of little white pearls. It is such a surprise I blink several times. I look away and then back to make sure I'm not

dreaming. I smile as I stare at them. I almost cry with happiness. I begin counting them to stifle my emotions. My eyesight blurs with wetness.

"Ah, so, Little Princess. There are eleven white pearls, all the same size, eleven for your age. Considering where they come from, and who they go to, they are the most beautiful gift I have ever seen. This is the pearl coast, and this village with the Mizu shrine is the home of pearl divers."

"Oh, Badi. How did they know? What should I say?"

"No words are needed, Royal One. They see you. They know. The story of your face when you first saw the pearls will be told a thousand times."

I tie the silk ends together and stuff the treasure in a pocket of my fur jacket. We have a delicious meal of roasted fish in the home of the mayor. Badiko seems to enjoy bossing everyone around. I am waited on by the mayor's three daughters, one my age and two older than I. We all four giggle when the hat worn by one of the elders falls off his head and lands in his rice bowl. I reach my hand into my pocket every chance I have, to feel the hard, round pearls in their hidden nest.

The village officials walk with us to the Mizu shrine. It is a simple flat rock covering a small arm of land, a tiny peninsula, jutting out into the ocean. There is no building or hut, only a thick wooden pole stuck in the ground, not even as tall as I. It's top and sides are covered with oyster shells. I walk to the rock, stand facing the shells, and clap my hands three times as instructed by Badiko. After giving thanks in this way to the sea for its bounty, I go back to the waiting people. All eyes are focused on a small boat coming to shore near us.

"The pearl divers are coming in from their work, Princess," Badiko says.

As the boat comes closer people jump out of it into the shallow water. They splash ashore. I can't believe what I see.

"Badiko! What is wrong with the divers? They are covered with pictures."

"Ah, so. Those are tattoos, Royal Child. The divers are covered with the pictures to frighten away bad fish. When the divers go deep for pearl oysters they meet aggressive fish. These enemies swim away from the pictures."

"Do the pictures ever fade away?"

"No, Princess. The tattoos are for life. On the elders they are a badge of honor. It is time now to get back on the litter and return to the palace. Are you ready?"

"Yes, I'm ready, Someday I'd like to come back here and watch the pearls be taken from the oysters."

"You will see everything, Princess. Climb up on the couch now so we can get started."

The carriers pick up the litter and the bouncing starts all over again. I decide I would rather travel by horseback, and will have to learn about horses and how to ride them. But first I have to figure out how to get Mother's permission.

The trip back to the palace goes quickly. Father meets us as we arrive late in the afternoon in a light rain. "Your mother would like to see you."

"Yes, Father." I take my bulky fur jacket off and give it to Badiko. She goes to our house to make it ready for the evening meal. I unlace and step out of my muddy footwear in the little room inside the door of my parents' house next to mine. Father slides the door open to the main room. I walk in behind him and take a deep breath to get ready for whatever lies ahead. My mother, elegant in red silk with white rice powder on her cheeks and cinnabar red on her lips, is sitting on a gold cushion near the center of the tea table, facing me.

TEA WITH MOTHER

"**W**ell, Jingu, did you have a pleasant journey?"

"Yes, Mother. Thank you."

"Were you treated well by everyone?"

"Yes, Mother. I was."

"Would you like tea?"

I have to be careful about my answer. Every time my mother serves tea to me she tries to make me give something up. Usually it is a thing I love, but sometimes it is even a choice I believe everyone should have. Once she tried to take Skoki away so I wouldn't get cat-sick. But I had never been sick, not from anything. Another time she wanted me to stay inside in the afternoon every day so I wouldn't get too tired by playing my games in the courtyard.

28   Tea with Mother

But I had never been too tired, not even one time. Would it be impolite to say no to the tea invitation? I think so.

"Yes, Mother. I'd like tea."

"Sit there beside your father. I understand you received a gift at Mizu. Tell us about it."

A servant sets a cup of hot tea in front of each of us. "The villagers gave me a present of eleven white pearls."

"Are they drilled for stringing?"

"No. They're just round and pretty."

"Will they be safe with you? Perhaps I should keep them for you. Let's take a look."

I don't know whether to feel relief that the pearls are in my jacket with Badiko, or fear that I might lose them. Does my mother want my pearls? She has pearls, big ones, of her own. I remember Chu Soy's advice, Think how to use words to guide the thoughts of the listener. What can I say? Her question is about the safety of the pearls. That's where I can use my words. And my unanswered question to Chu Soy about who could have suggested the trip to Mizu — maybe I can use words about that.

"Yes, Mother. My pearls will be safe with me. No one could love them as I do. You mustn't worry about my little pearls. I'm so grateful to you and father for letting me go to the Mizu shrine. I can't thank you enough, you and all those who made the trip possible."

"I understand, daughter, although I would still like to see the pearls."

"Of course. They are in my jacket in my house. I'll bring them the next time I visit."

"I see. Well, you were always a stubborn child. Nothing new there. Drink your tea now. We have important company arriving soon."

I drink half of my tea and stand up. Father walks me to the door and kisses my forehead. He gives a little chuckle and kisses me again. I giggle and run barefoot out of his vestibule and onto the short path between our houses, clutching my shoes in both hands. The guards see me coming and open my door so I can run into my house.

Badiko is tending the stove. "Did you have a nice visit, Princess?"

"Yes, Badi. Where's my jacket?"

"On the bed in your room. Wash the mud off your feet, Royal One, and sit for a hot meal."

I dash into my room and scoop up my jacket. I hurry to the courtyard door and slide it open. "I'll be right back."

Running to the fish pond through the drizzle, I fetch the silk packet out of the jacket pocket. I lean over the wall around the pool and plunge the packet as far under the surface as I can, until my shoulder is in the water. I touch the floor of the pool with my fingers and feel the plants that grow there. I let go of my treasure. For a moment I stay bent over, my hand still under water, to learn by feeling if the packet will rise up. It stays put. My pearls are safe. I go in the house and clean up with hot water Badiko has ready..

Badiko is older than my mother and knows a lot about normal people. My mother knows all about Imperial Court people. I'm not sure Badiko will talk to me about the Nobles, but I'm very curious. "Badi, why do some mothers love their children and some do not?"

"Ah, so. I think all mothers love their children, Royal Child. But some mothers have trouble showing their love. They have no easy way to express it. Perhaps a mother may feel weak if she shows love. A mother always cares, sometimes too much. A mother can be protective of a child and still not show much love."

"That's my mother. She's scared of everything I do. She's protective, but her reasons are silly, like me getting cat-sick, or not sitting near the fish pond because she thinks I might drown in that puddle."

"Ah, so. Those are forms of mother-love, Princess. Those are her ways of saying she loves you. Mothers can show love in very different ways."

"I think she wants my pearls."

"Oh, Princess Jingu. I don't think so. She has her own white pearls."

"But suppose I'm right, Badi. She asked twice to see them."

"Ah, so. That is interesting, Royal One. We should ask Chu Soy to think about that. You know, suppose a mother loves her daughter so much that she has to have some little thing the daughter adores. Then the mother can have a bit of the daughter with her anytime, day or night, without asking. She can look at it and touch it and pretend it's her daughter."

"Badi, you make me feel cruel for what I said about my mother wanting the pearls. Please don't tell Chu Soy I think that way. He would scold me."

"Chu Soy is not going to tell you how women should think, Princess."

"You're right. I'm thinking of a way to test your idea. Suppose I tell Mother I don't like the pearls anymore and she can have them. If she takes them it means she really wants the pearls, not because she loves me. What do you think she'll do?"

"Ah, so. You are one clever child, Princess, to plan like that. Hah! Lady Katsuraki had better watch out for her little daughter. Finish your meal now. Then I'll brush your hair. Are you weary from sitting on that bouncing couch all day?"

"Yes, Badi, I'm tired. Thank you for taking such good care of me today."

"You are a joy to travel with, Little Princess. You'll make many trips, I'm sure."

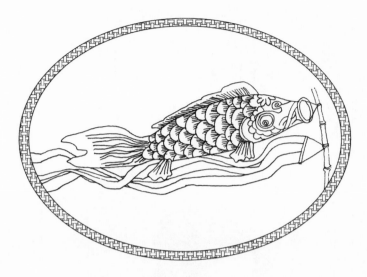

THE KNOT-HOLE

I continue to learn my lessons, month after month, while cooped up like a chicken. I copy and remember all the Chinese figures Chu Soy draws with a brush, and can read much of his writing. He tells stories about things that have happened in China, and he explains why they occurred. Then he asks me what I would do to make things better. He gives me choices. Against floods I choose to build thick walls to keep the water back, not make everybody move to the top of a mountain. Against enemies I also build a wall, a thin one, and train my army behind it. My teacher makes his questions into an interesting game with many choices for each problem, and more difficult each time.

34 The Knot-hole

After the noon meal on a day following my twelfth birthday I run into the courtyard for my exercises and hear boys cheering. The unusual noise comes from the other side of the board fence, from the next courtyard. The wall is several times my height and has no place to look through. I get close and stare at each board. I see a knot and poke it with my finger. It's rough and raspy like Skoki's tongue. It wiggles but won't fall out of the board. I pick up a small stone and tap it against the knot. Now there is an opening as big as an apple. I look through it.

There are boys my size running zigzag on the brown dirt field. They chase a large ball. They kick it and yell. I count ten bare-chested boys. Each wears a breechcloth and a white headband with loose ends that flap up and down. I watch, fascinated, as they struggle to kick the ball along the ground. Their bodies flash and their arms spin for balance.

One boy yells as he goes after the ball. "I'll catch up to you, Ichiro."

Soon I realize the one called Ichiro is the most daring. He is going after the ball when it looks like he shouldn't, when others have it under control. No one charges like he does. I study him. His face is composed, even at the most thrilling times. He has wide shoulders and muscled legs. I feel a terrible urge to play or yell or run. My feet jump off the ground without my telling them. I press my face against the knot-hole.

Now the ball is just between Ichiro and the other good player. They each run at it. I see a flash of Ichiro's white teeth. The race will be close. I cannot contain myself.

"Go Ichiro, go!" I yell in a high-pitched scream through the knot-hole in the fence.

The game stops instantly. The ten boys stand as still as tree stumps. Their puzzled faces turn toward the fence. I watch as Ichiro breaks away and walks slowly to the wall. His eyes scan left and right. His gaze lands on the portion of my face pressed against the large knothole. I feel like shrinking into the ground. I know my face is all red. I know I should turn away but I cannot.

He is an arm's length away when he speaks. "Hello."

"I did not mean to stop your game. Please continue playing."

A pause. Then, "Are you Princess Jingu?"

"Yes, how did you guess my name?"

"You speak differently from other girls. Your voice is the sing-song of the Chinese teacher, like music. Everyone knows Jingu has the teacher Chu Soy."

His voice is strong, but polite and warm. "I see. Well, you are right."

"May I ask how you knew my name to yell it so loudly, or were you calling to someone else?"

"It's the only name I heard while watching your game."

"I see. Well, I am Ichiro. It is an honor and pleasure to meet Your Highness. I've often wondered where you are hiding. No one in the palace will say."

"I'm not hiding. That's nonsense. But I'm not allowed friends, not even visitors. I've never heard you play in the next courtyard before."

"This is our first game next to your courtyard. Do you mind?"

"Oh, no. Please continue as long and as often as you like."

I see his smile. His face is kind. He bends down to pick up the knot lying beneath the hole. I back away from the fence an arm's length. Now he has one eye against the knothole and studies all of me before asking, "Did this fall out?"

"No. I hit it with a stone to make it pop out." I hear a clamor of yells behind him. "Your friends are calling you."

Ichiro backs away to signal his friends and stick the wood knot in his waistband before asking, "Will you be here if I come back another day?"

I move close to the knothole to look at his serious face. "I'll be here."

"Princess, do you know the song of the bluebird?"

"Of course."

"If I whistle the notes in the evening, like this," he whistles, "can you come to our meeting place here?"

"Yes," I say, feeling strangely light-headed and short of breath. I trust him. He is like a little mountain, solid and unshakable. Finally, I may have a friend. "But you must promise not to let anyone know you've seen me. My mother, Lady Katsuraki, would stop us."

"It is our secret, I promise you."

The Bluebird Sings

A few days later I hear Ichiro's bluebird whistle calling for the first time. I fly out of my house like a shooting star. He is there at the fence, on the other side. In the day's last light we look at each other through the knothole before we speak. I see only his face.

"I can't stay long," he says. "My father is very strict."

"I know what you mean. My mother is the same."

He is curious, "What are you going to do, I mean besides being a princess? Will you become a Court Lady?"

"No, probably not a Court Lady. Maybe a teacher or a soldier."

"Oh, I see. Do you write on paper?"

"Yes, of course." I wonder why he asks. I see his smile.

"So do I. Will you write your name on paper and give it to me next time?"

I know he is not royalty. There are no princes named Ichiro. Nor could there be a royal prince about fourteen so fearless as this Ichiro. The servants would speak of him. But if he can write Chinese he is from a high family. "Why do you wish my writing?" I ask.

"First tell me if you will write your name for me."

"Yes, I will. Now tell me why you want it."

"To have something from you. I must go now. Goodbye until the bluebird sings again."

I watch through the knothole as he grows smaller and smaller. But I feel something inside me, a friendship, growing bigger and bigger. I go indoors.

Badiko is waiting. "Princess, did I hear you talking outside?"

"Yes, Badi. I have a friend. We talk through a hole in the fence."

"Ah, so. Your mother would not permit this, Royal One. If it continues we could both be in trouble with her."

"Who would tell her, Badi? It's a secret. He's smart and very brave."

"Ah, so, Princess Jingu. I knew this day would come. What is the boy's name?"

"He is called Ichiro."

"Ah, oh."

"Oh what?" I ask as she looks at my face with new interest.

"Nothing, Royal Child. Have your friend. But be ready for trouble."

I coil my piece of paper up smaller than the hole in the fence and fasten the roll with a thin brown ribbon. When the bluebird calls a few days later I rush to the fence. Ichiro watches me run toward him. Before I slide the paper through the knothole I stand next to the fence returning his stare.

He smiles at me. "Well, Princess. Please let me see it."

"Here it is, Ichiro." I push the rolled-up page of paper through the hole and then speak close to the fence. "May I ask something of you?"

"Yes, Your Highness."

His voice is sweet. I know I am blushing and my face is all red. I put my hand up against the apple-sized hole so he can't see me. Then I take my hand away and put my head to one side of the hole, where I'm hidden from his view.

"Can you bring me something of many colors?"

"Yes, Princess Jingu. Let's think of what it can be."

"Like tree leaves just before winter," I suggest to him. "There are red colors, along with yellow and orange. I have no trees here, no such colors."

I look through the hole.

He is deep in thought, staring at the base of the fence on his side. He looks up, eyes wide with excitement. "I know! I'll bring you a feather from the Emperor's parrot. Those tail feathers have every color in the rainbow."

"A parrot?"

"Yes. The giant bird was a gift to the Emperor from pirates who came from the south. Its name is Okime. Don't worry. There are plenty of feathers. One will not be missed."

"Ichiro, I don't want you getting into trouble over a silly feather."

"No, no. It's no trouble. I go in the cage and feed the parrot. He likes me. A rainbow feather falls out every once in a while. The next one is yours."

"What do you feed Okime?"

He laughs before saying, "Live crickets."

"You are teasing me."

"No. Parrots are birds, and birds eat live insects. The Emperor's parrot likes live crickets, big ones. I know where to capture the biggest, up in the foothills. I put them in a cricket box woven of straw. Now that I think of it, I am the official Cricket-Catcher and Parrot-Feeder of the Royal Court."

I laugh out loud at his words and his way of making fun of what he does. He laughs at me, and then we both laugh so hard we lean against the fence on each side, toward each other.

I am the happiest girl in the world.

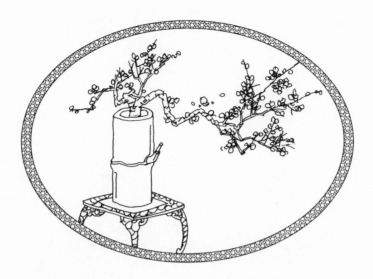

PALACE GOSSIP

Sometime after this, when I am fourteen and know Ichiro well from our many talks at the fence, a new servant, Kosiko, arrives. She is to carry meals from the palace kitchen to my rooms for me, Badiko, and my teachers.

Badiko tells me, "She is sixteen, Royal Child, and has been trying to get this job for two years. She's heard the stories about you and your studies, and about how lonely your childhood has been. Kosiko is very smart and knows most of the palace gossip."

"Can we trust someone like that, Badi?"

"Ah, so. Perhaps, Princess. You are always testing ideas and people. Think of a test for her. Here she comes."

I study her as she looks at Skoki curled up on a corner table, crosses the room and bows three

times. She has a friendly face and steady eyes. She wears a coarse, dark-blue kimono and black cotton foot-covering. I ask in a kind voice, "Kosiko, if you heard palace stories that I had a secret friend would you tell me of the gossip?"

She kneels before me, head bowed low. Her kimono-covered knees rest on the woven-straw floor. I can barely hear her words. "Yes, Highness. My life is yours. If you asked me to tell you I would speak."

Her voice is frightened, unsteady. I am curious. "Do you know of any such gossip?"

"Yes, Highness."

I am alarmed. "What is this palace gossip, Kosiko?"

"Highness, the Chief General of the Imperial Army has a son who may be sent away by a Royal Command."

"What is the name of the son, and how many know of this?"

She puts both hands to her face, bows deeply, and whispers. "It is Ichiro, Your Highness. Many Court persons speak of the friendship."

I feel a sudden weakness. I close my eyes. My mother. She will cause Ichiro to be sent away. "How did they find out about Ichiro?"

"There are more spies in the palace than I can count, Highness."

I am so upset my head hurts. "Where do you learn these things?"

"In the palace kitchens, Highness, from Royal Servants, from soldiers, from people who listen through paper walls and see everything."

I look across the room. "Chu Soy, did you hear this?"

"Yes, Heavenly One." He nods at her. "Kosiko may be the very best spy."

During our next talk at the fence knothole I tell Ichiro, "Our secret, after these two wonderful years, is gone. My mother knows. You could be sent away, Ichi. We must stop meeting until the danger is over."

He frowns. "I wonder who Lady Katsuraki talks to about me without my father knowing. I wish we could find out."

I think of Kosiko. "I have an idea. My new servant hears everything. She is like a spy. Maybe she can find out who my mother is scheming with. Then we can figure out a way to stop their snooping. Could it be someone in the Imperial Court plotting against your father?"

"Plotting against my father could be treason, Jingu."

"Well, let's find out. We might be doing the Court a big favor. I'll see Kosiko right now. Let's meet here in the morning."

Badiko sends for Kosiko. She comes running, and follows me out to the courtyard. We sit on the fishpond wall, just above my hidden pearls.

"Kosi, I have a dangerous, very important job for you. You can refuse it and I will understand. Listen carefully. Lady Katsuraki speaks with a minister in the Imperial Court about Ichiro and me. I think that minister then speaks to the Prime Minister, Count Takechi, and tells him, without saying my name, that Ichiro is causing trouble in a family. I need to know who the minister is so Ichiro's father can talk to him. Do you understand?"

"Yes, Highness." Her head is up, eyes shining. She is smiling. Her face turns red after looking at my eyes.

I feel a surge of hope. "Kosi, you naughty girl. You know something."

"Yes, Highness. But let me make sure. There is a minister. His servants are doing their laundry with the other tax minister servants at the wash place. Tell me what to do."

"Can you find out now and come back tonight?"

"I think so, Highness."

"Good. I'll wait for you."

A tax minister. There are dozens, maybe even one hundred of these officials. I don't know any of them. Father does, but that's no help. And Mother knows every one of them and their wives. Maybe there's no treason against Japan involved, just an old man my mother has talked into warning the Prime Minister about something that isn't true. I go in the house and wait for Kosiko.

The door rattles and is opened by the guards. Kosi rushes in, breathless again. We go into the garden and sit on the fishpond wall. She whispers in my ear. "It is Tax Minister Tatsuda. He speaks to Count Takechi about Ichiro and suggests he be promoted and sent away."

"Goodness, Kosi. You learned all this at the wash place in such a short time?"

"No, Highness. I knew before, but had to make sure. Everyone has servants with big ears. The servants know everything about almost every Royal Person."

"If you are right, Kosi, there will be a gift for you. Thick earmuffs, perhaps. Ha! Thank you for acting so quickly. Goodnight."

She bows and runs into the house. I hear the corridor palace door open and close. I sleep well and dream about Kosiko telling me all of the secrets of all the Court Royals, but in a strange language. I wake up laughing.

In the morning I wait at the fence for Ichiro, pacing back and forth. My empty teacup is on the fishpond wall above the pearls. Finally I hear his whistle, the silly parrot whistle he's learned from Okime. I reach my hand through the fence and wave my fingers. He runs to touch me. "Ichi, it's Tax Minister Tatsuda. He talks to Count Takechi about you. Takechi will see that you get a promotion and be sent away."

"Tatsuda, that old busy-body. Never, never, never. Wait here, Jingu. I'll fix this before you can drink a cup of hot tea. Will you wait?"

"Of course. Hurry"

I carry my teacup in for Badiko to fill. Chu Soy is at the study table. "I will not be long, Honorable Teacher."

He winks at me.

Ichiro is gone longer than a hot drink of tea. He runs to the fence. He takes a deep breath. "My father is talking with Minister Tatsuda now. I think Tatsuda will retire soon. Maybe today. Hah! Then I think there will be a quick meeting at noon today between my father and Takechi. I'm telling you, Jingu, every time your name comes up, or is even thought of, things happen. I feel like I'm in a whirlpool."

"You make things happen, Ichi."

"There's more, Princess. My military field training will be completed soon. I am then to become an assistant captain of the military someplace here in the palace."

"That's very good news. You deserve a promotion."

"Also, I heard talk in my father's office that you are to have an elderly man-servant to shield you against men who admire you. Lady Katsuraki is no longer the boss of your life. I think the old Emperor looks out for you."

"Really? I wonder why, Ichi. What do you think?"

"Well, you read and write more Chinese than just about anyone except Chu Soy. You study and learn more than anyone I ever heard of. Maybe there are plans all made out for your future."

"But I never see anything. Mother keeps me cooped up here like a chicken."

"Jingu, suppose that's part of the plan. The teachers fill your head with knowledge before you travel everywhere and see all of the confusion outside of your coop."

He is right. Chu Soy has said almost the same thing. "The question now, Ichi, is when does my head get full? When do I get to travel?"

Ichiro leans close to our fence hole. "You'll see. Changes are coming."

Good News

A few mornings later Badiko drags me out of my bed-furs before sunrise. "Princess, wake up. An Assistant Minister will be here in three hours. You must be ready to talk with him."

I have no idea what is happening. Badi and Kosi wash me and work on my hair. A new orange silk kimono is fitted on with a gold sash. I am ready. The palace door opens to admit a tall, dark, young man in courtly dress.

"I am Sinoto, Your Highness. I come from the office of Prime Minister Takechi. You are to have a man-servant. We wish to discuss this matter with you after the noon meal today. I will escort you to the Ministry at that time."

"You are most kind. I do not need a man-servant, but I am honored at the invitation. I am also happy to walk across the palace grounds."

Sinoto returns later in the day. I am escorted across the packed dirt paths in the palace and between buildings. It is easy to see that Sinoto is not used to walking with a girl. I am wearing wooden platform shoes with high steps to keep my white-stocking feet out of the mud. I have to take very short steps to stay in the shoes. He gets ahead and stops, skips up to me, turns this way and that. He is polite and, as is the custom when observing a Royal Person, tries not to look at my eyes. I laugh and his face turns red.

I smell the horses and hear their hooves stomp in the military stables. We come to a building as tall as three men with a large sliding door above steps as wide as my house. The wooden door is covered with carvings of dragons painted red. It is opened from the inside as we climb the wide steps. We slip out of our footwear and are ushered into the Prime Minister's office. He is the most powerful man in Japan next to the Emperor. Count Takechi's face is old and wise, wrinkled and peaceful. His hair is white on top of his head and below his chin. The black kimono he wears glows with the finest silk. He rises to bow three times. I am taller than he is. I return the courtesy and try not to stand to my full height. I see a painted scroll hanging on the far wall with three white herons flying, one above the other, against a blue sky. A miniature pine tree grows from an earthen pot below the scroll. I have difficulty pulling my gaze away from the gracefulness. We sit on red floor cushions around a dark wood tea table.

"Ah, Princess Jingu. I was not properly advised of your appearance. You may become the most attractive member of our clan. I bow my head once more to your beauty."

"I am disarmed, Count Takechi, by your flattery."

"How elegantly you speak, Princess. Your teachers have had much success. Are you perhaps disarmed enough to accept my offer of a man-servant to protect you against men as impressed with you as I am? "

"Thank you. But, no. I am properly guarded in my isolation. My greatest need is for friends my age."

"Young lady, dear Princess. Your isolation is about to end. You are to enter the Court. Many young people, Royal, military, and academic, will surround you. The idea of a man-servant requires consideration if only for that reason."

I can not believe my ears. My world is opening. I see him move one hand in a flicker. Two servants rush from the shadows to pour tea into delicate, hand-painted cups from far-away China. We drink.

"Count Takechi, I wish to continue my studies but do not need another servant. I would rather accept a teacher of military affairs, perhaps a retired general."

His lined face breaks into a smile. "Good! That is acceptable. I see there is a bit of proud warrior in you. Most unusual. You will enter the Court during the spring festival. One day each week you shall be a teacher to the young Royals. Is that agreeable with you?"

"Yes, Count Takechi. I am honored to accept your guidance."

He drinks from his teacup, holding it in the fingertips of both hands. "Now, Princess, are there any matters you wish to discuss with me?"

I think of the secret behind the mirror. Is he going to say something linked to those words? Perhaps he knows the secret and wants me to ask what it means. Or, does he think I will ask that Ichiro not be sent away? I study his face but see nothing that tells me whether or not he likes me. Then I think of Chu Soy's favorite saying, that each word you speak is a treasure given away forever. "No," I say. "Thank you for asking."

"One more announcement," he says with a twinkle in his eyes, "General Hamado's son, Ichiro, will be here with me as assistant to Sinoto. It is arranged." He sets his teacup down, smiles at me and nods at Sinoto.

Such good news! I stand and bow to the Prime Minister, shaking a little in excitement, before following Sinoto out through the sliding door. Ichiro must learn the good news from me.

On the way back to my house I want to hurry, but cannot. My stilted wooden shoes keep my feet out of the mud but slow me down. Sinoto sees my frustration but says nothing as he tries not to look at me. He leaves me with my guards at the corridor door. I enter and change quickly with Badiko's help. I run to the courtyard fence and stand in front of the knothole. I'm still shaking with the good news.

Oh, Ichi, where are you? I purse my lips and try to whistle the bluebird song. No sound comes out. My eyes feel wet. I wait and wait. Nothing. The sun goes down. I run back in the house and pick up a flaming oil lamp made of fired clay. Carefully, I carry the lamp outside to the fence and hold the flame up to the knothole. Ichi, please come.

Soon I hear a far-away whistle. It's a bluebird. It's Ichiro! Such joy floods into me I cry out without meaning to. "Ichi!"

I see him running to the fence. "Yes, Jingu. I am here."

I bubble over with words. "Everything we did worked for us. Takechi is protecting us. You are to work in his ministry with Sinoto. I am to teach the Royal Children. Our friendship is safe."

"Hah, the old Emperor favors you. Now you know how things work in the Palace."

KNOWLEDGE

In my sixteenth year Father gives me a Mongol pony with shaggy brown hair. I name him Kuri and keep him in the military stables. He minds me and comes when I call. That's more than I can say for my white cat. Skoki is seven now and still acts like she owns me. I wonder if there is a lesson to be learned from my two pets. Kuri is a big, sweet pony who waits for me to tell him what to do. Skoki is not much bigger than Kuri's hoof. She's sweet too, but she just sits around telling me to feed her, let her out, let her in, stroke her, and hold her in my lap. I have learned rom her that little things can sometimes require more attention than great big ones.

Ichiro and I meet on the palace grounds and in my classrooms for long talks. My lessons continue with teachers of spoken history, of map-making, soil fertility, ailment cures, and, of course, all the things Chu Soy teaches. During my study of logic he gives me a hint about the times ahead.

"Your curiosity will bring you more knowledge than most people have, Heavenly One."

"How can you tell? That's like knowing the future."

"It is not complicated, Princess. The more you know about history, the better you can guess what might happen next. Even recent history. A fishing boat will not go out in a storm because there are stories told about people who went out in rough weather and never came back. Those are the lessons of history."

"When I was ten I wondered why you talked so much about events that happened long ago. I remember thinking it was too late to fix the mistakes, so why should we waste time talking about them?"

Chu Soy hides his hands in the wide cuffs of his long-sleeved gown, left hand in the right sleeve, right hand in the left. He smiles at me. "Ah, Princess, when you were ten I sometimes saw that question in your face during lessons."

"I don't remember making a face, Chu Soy. Are you teasing me?"

"No, Heavenly One. A teacher reads a student's face. Your face was like a mirror of my words as I spoke the lessons to you. I could almost always tell, by watching your expression, when you were learning and when you were daydreaming."

"I thank you, Chu Soy, more every day, for speaking your wise words."

"Today's lessons are ended, Royal One. I understand you have an appointment to talk with the Emperor tomorrow to discuss your activities in the Court. Rest your mind now. Go out into the sunlight."

I skip into the courtyard and sit on the wall around the pond. I face the fence where I first looked through the knot-hole. There is now a door in the fence, one I can use to visit the guarded courtyard attached to mine.

The next morning there is a great fuss over my hair, my kimono, and my foot-covering. Everything has to be just perfect. My mother and Badiko guide the nervous servants in preparing my appearance, while Kosiko is the only one who keeps a steady head. After the mid-day meal my parents, also dressed for the audience, walk with me to the main rooms of the Imperial Palace. Members of the Royal Household meet us at the little bridge in front of the entrance. They escort us inside the clay-brick building, thickly roofed with thatched straw. We enter a waiting room where Mother energetically greets others who also wait. Father, as usual, is very quiet. When it is our turn to see the Emperor my parents are asked to wait for my return, and I, very much surprised, am led into the audience without them.

The old Emperor is seated on a floor cushion before a large, low table. He smiles and waves me forward with a weak gesture. "Princess Jingu, you are my pride and joy in your studies. Come sit across from me. Let my old eyes take in your youth. Does your progress continue with your teachers?"

"Yes, Your Majesty."

He looks down at the table. A servant soundlessly comes from a corner of the room, drops to her knees, and pours tea into two cups. She sets one cup in front of the Emperor and one before me. After he raises his cup from the table I lift mine. We drink. The servant leaves the room and we are alone.

The Emperor speaks slowly, looking at me over his cup. "At a time not yet chosen you are to be named the Imperial Princess. I had that vision on your tenth birthday, and wrote the Imperial Princess secret blessing in my gift to you, beneath the birthday mirror. What is this? What does your big smile mean?"

"Your Majesty, I pulled the mirror out of the holder to find out if I could see the back of my head on the reverse side of the mirror. I saw the writing and have kept the secret for six years, wondering what it means."

"Excellent, Princess. Now there are other secrets for you to keep. What I have to say is about Japan, about our beloved country, about the many years ahead. I am old and wish for the Exalted Sleep.

Sometime after I make my Heavenly Journey you are to become the wife of my successor, the next emperor."

I bow my dizzy head. I think first of Ichiro. But that is selfish. I must think first of my country, about Japan. "I shall be ready, Your Majesty."

"I know that, dear Princess. For now, and for your safety, we must keep this decision between us. Tell no one. There are jealous people in the Court who might wish to hurt you, or do worse, if they knew. Only we two, the Chosen One, and the Prime Minister know. I am telling you this now as a precaution, in case you have any serious romantic ideas, and because you have studied so hard these many years. For those who ask what we are doing in here today, Princess Jingu, you are hereby appointed an Assistant Minister of Education. There are, as you know, hundreds of assistant ministers."

"It is a great honor for me, Your Majesty. Thank you."

"You'll meet all the people in those offices. You have to know, Jingu, that although your future Captain Ichiro will one day be a great General of the Imperial Army, he will not be your husband. You must accept that."

"I . . . I accept that, Your Majesty."

"Good. I am truly proud of you. Now go, and stay well."

Still facing him, still breathless with shock, I rise and back away, turning as the door slides open. My parents come to me with eager faces, Mother leaning forward to look into my eyes as if words are written in them.

"Well?" she asks.

"I am an Assistant Minister of Education."

"Oh," Mother whispers. "Is that all?"

We walk home in silence. I can't wait to be alone, to think by myself. I part politely from my parents at my corridor door. Badiko sees that I am troubled and helps me out of my kimono without speaking. I dress in my courtyard clothes and carry Skoki outside. I sit on the ground with my back against the fishpond wall, where no one can see me. Skoki purrs in my lap. "Oh, please, please, Ichiro," I cry, "never forget the song of the bluebird."

My wonderful new secret lies buried in my sadness.

A Gift

The day after my audience with the Emperor one of Mother's servants rushes into the study room to announce, "Princess, Lady Katsuraki will be here shortly to visit you."

Chu Soy picks up our lesson papers from the table and drags a floor cushion across the room. He sits with his back against the wall, the papers in his lap. Badiko fluffs a pillow and places it on the floor at the head of the table, next to where I'm sitting. She and Kosiko reach down on each side of me to adjust my hair.

"Badi, do you know why Mother wants to visit?"

"Ah, so, Royal One. I don't know. There are many smiles around us today. Maybe your mother will bring you a smile."

68　A Gift

I try to remember Mother smiling. No memory appears. It is not that she frowns, but her face just never changes expression. I wonder if the white rice powder on her face would fall off if she smiled. But I guess not. It stays on when she talks. Perhaps Mother was not satisfied with my explanation of the audience with the Emperor. I don't think I can fool her if she asks a lot of questions. She must believe something important happened and is coming here to ask about it in her clever way. I make up my mind to change the subject if she becomes too persistent.

A moment later Mother, wearing a black silk kimono bunched tightly at the waist with a grey sash, walks in. I get up from the study table and bow to her.

She is smiling. How did Badi know? "Jingu, I want to congratulate you. The Emperor has let your father and me know that he is proud of you. I must say you have made a good impression in the Court."

"Thank you, Mother."

"I bring a gift for you — two gifts, really. Here."

She holds out one hand with a small, black cloth packet in her palm.

I take it and kneel at the table to unfold the cloth layers. I think about the gifts I've received. It was always Father who brought me presents. Of course, Mother chooses my clothing, or tells Badiko what to have made for me. But those are not gifts. Just getting a gift from Mother is a surprise. What can it be? I lift the last flap of silk to reveal the gift. For a moment I think my eyes deceive me. I am almost speechless with shock.

There are two large white pearls, perfectly matched. I rise and turn to look at her. "Mother, I . . ."

"Never mind. I've had the pair for a while, intending to give them to you as Mother and Daughter pearls. One is me; one is you. Today, because you are so grown up, they are Two-Women pearls."

"Oh, Mother." I rush to her and we clasp each other tightly.

"That's enough for now. Enjoy your pearls, Jingu. I must go."

Mother leaves. I go out to the fishpond and bring my wet packet of Mizu pearls up from the bottom. I open the silk folds and dry my little treasures on a clean cloth. Moments later I answer a knock at the corridor door. It is Ichiro.

"Welcome, Ichi. Please come in for tea."

He visits with me in my study room while Badiko rests in her alcove and Kosiko heats tea water on the clay stove. The pearls from Mizu lie in the silk holding Mother's gift. "Look at the pearls my mother gave me. They're the same color and luster as those from Mizu."

He picks up one of the large pearls. "What will you do with them? These would make fantastic earrings for you."

"I've thought of earrings, but I'll wait a few years before doing that."

"What about the little ones?"

That question has bothered me since I was eleven. Sitting at the pond, I've shown the pearls to Ichiro several times, but we've never talked about what to do with them. "I don't know, Ichi. No one has given me a good suggestion."

"Princess, do you remember the knot from the fence, the one you popped out to make a hole so you could watch our game of kick-ball?"

"I remember, of course. What about the knot?"

"Well, I picked it up that first day while we were talking. And I kept it. About a year ago I gave it to a craftsman to polish and make into a keepsake for you. He made an oval from the center of the knot. I didn't tell you about it because I was not sure anything good would come from a knot of wood."

"Ichi, it's not like you to have a secret. Where is the keepsake?"

He blushes. "I have it here."

"Well?"

He reaches into his kimono and brings out a slim, dark object the size of a small butterfly wing. "It's yours, Jingu. But it's just wood."

I take the oval in my fingers. It is perfectly formed, smooth, and highly polished. The color is a dark, dark brown. I am sure there is nothing like it in all the world. "It is so unusual, Ichi." I set it on the table and space my little pearls around the edge of the oval to see what the combination looks like.

"That is beautiful," Ichiro says.

I like the way the white pearls and the dark polished knot contrast. "I agree. It would make a nice brooch. Mother has a jeweler who can put everything together. That would settle the problem of my eleven pearls. Thank you, Ichi."

My Future

I ride Kuri every day. Ichiro often goes with me on his horse. We ride fast on the paths between the wide rice fields, then go slowly up into the green mountain foothills. My Court guards and assistants ride nearby, always within view.

One day when we are resting the horses near a stream and my nearby attendants are letting their ponies drink, Ichiro comments, "Jingu, you don't talk as much since your audience with the Emperor."

"My life is not my own, Ichi. It belongs to our country. You, as a soldier sworn to serve Japan, must know the feeling."

"Oh, yes, Princess. I know. But you're a girl, not a soldier. Are you so quiet because of something you have to do that bothers you?"

How well he knows me! What should I tell him? It isn't fair to leave my best friend completely in the dark. But I can't go back on my word to the Emperor. As Ichiro tightens the strap on his pony, I look down at my feet in their deer-hide covering. One foot belongs to a girl who has everything she could want, the best and bravest friend, the finest teachers, proud parents, every comfort. The other foot is attached to a solemn vow to begin living a different life, to marry a stranger when I am told to do so. That part of me is no longer a girl. It is strange and I'm not sure what to call it. I have a foot in each of two worlds, one of them secret. I guess this makes me extra careful about my words when I'm talking, even to Ichiro.

"Ichi," I say gently, looking directly at him and waiting until he realizes that what I am about to say is more important than any words in our five years of friendship. "I belong to Japan."

He looks down at his feet in their riding boots. "I see. What will become of you?"

"I'm going to be whatever is needed. A teacher now, and later there will be other responsibilities. Maybe someday I'll be a soldier, or a priestess, or just a Court Lady."

"Jingu, I think you'll be what you want to be."

"Well, not any time soon. For now I want to begin helping the clans get along with each other. That would be a good start. There is too much fighting between our many clans."

"Hey, wait! That's the work of the military. We have bad clans who have built high walls and fences between each other. They've been fighting for a hundred years. That's no place for a teacher."

"You are making me tell you one of my secrets, Ichi. All right — here it is. I'm sixteen now. I know what I want — to be a leader. I've been trained to be a leader. Whatever else happens, I will be a leader."

He stares at me. "Jingu, when you talk so forcefully my scalp tingles. There's a fire in you. The words are so powerful. Do you mean them?"

"Yes, Ichi. Of course. Do you remember the first words I ever spoke to you?"

"I'm thinking. I'm thinking. Was it . . ."

"It was, 'Go, Ichiro. Go.' I yelled it through the knothole during your game on the other side of my courtyard fence."

"Ha! I remember that. You sure made me go. I'm still going."

"You're funny sometimes. We need to make things go in the right direction, but not like the travel of a snail. Our leaders are so old and slow. They creak like dead trees in the wind. What they do is good, but it's not enough. New leaders, men and women with fresh visions, are needed. People our age are still too young to gain office, to become ministers and generals, but we can get ready. We can travel, and listen, and learn. Ichi, will you help me in these endeavors no matter what happens between us?"

Ichiro drops his horse's reins to the ground. He places one hand on his sword hilt and bows deeply to me. "Princess, my life and honor are yours to command." He straightens up. "But we are only two."

He is so grand. For five years, from the first day we talked at the fence, he has been my best friend. I trust him like my own hands. He may always be my best friend, even though I shall one day, perhaps soon, become Empress of Japan. I feel my eyes get wet. "So? How many does it take to lead?"

"One, General Jingu," he teases. "But seriously, there have to be followers, tens of thousands. Our people will not leave their rice fields for military duty just to tear down those fences. Not unless there are very strong reasons for doing so."

"Ichi, we must unify our clans and stop fighting each other here on our own islands. Is that a strong enough reason for the people to make a brief sacrifice?"

"It is. Are you thinking that far ahead?"

"Yes, I'm planning ahead. Everyone who produces food, from the land or the sea, must pay a fair tax to the Emperor. The Emperor pays the ministers, and the ministers assure the peace between all of the tax-payers. We don't need fences and walls."

"I like the way you speak. Is that what the old Emperor told you?"

"No, that's what Chu Soy has been telling me since he first entered my house ten years ago." In a way Ichiro has guessed the truth. It is the Emperor who attracted Chu Soy to Japan, gave him a house, sent him to my study table, and provided him with a high station for life.

"I think you're right, Jingu. Treating people fairly seems to do more good than using force. But some leaders don't see that."

It is good to hear Ichiro, trained in the military, say those words. "We have to point the way and work with those people dedicated to peaceful progress."

"When do you think we can start looking on both sides of those clan fences?"

"Well, we're both about to begin our new official jobs. I think we should begin looking on both sides now, begin meeting people from throughout Japan. After all, who knows more about making friends through a fence than you and I?"

Historical Note

The fourteenth Emperor of Japan married Imperial Princess Jingu in her last teen year. He was more than twice her age. The ceremony took place during the third year of his reign. Tragedy struck when, a few years later, he died from a battle wound. The young widow Empress Jingu then became the reigning monarch of her country.

Right after the Emperor's death and before she gave birth to their son Odin, Jingu performed a mighty task. She led her army across the ocean into Korea. There she achieved a lasting peace without fighting a single battle. She immediately returned to Japan, leaving a small army in Korea to protect her new friends from invaders. Empress Jingu sent ambassadors to the capitol cities of China. These Japanese officials brought new ideas, new weapons, and fresh culture back to Japan. Jingu began the introduction of the first written Japanese language. She raised young Odin to become one of the most revered of all Japan's 124 Imperial Emperors. His name today, 1,600 years later, is in shrines in every large and small city in Japan.

Before her marriage to the fourteenth Emperor in A.D. 356, Princess Jingu was elevated to Imperial Princess Jingu. The inscription behind the mirror given Jingu on her tenth birthday in this story shows one way this advance from "Princess" to "Imperial Princess" might have been arranged. Her marriage to the Emperor gave her the title of Empress. Following her many later successes at governing her country Jingu was again elevated, this time by her ministers. She is named in Japan's history as Grand Empress Jingu.

There is one place where we can read an actual description of Jingu when she was still a young princess. It is in a book called "Nihongi, *Chronicles of Japan from the*

Earliest Times to A.D. 697." Here are the words translated from the writing in Chinese:

> "While still young she was intelligent and shrewd, and her appearance was of such blooming beauty that the Prince her father was filled with wonder."

Another translation from "Nihongi" tells of Empress Jingu's first speech to her ministers. These were not church ministers, but were office-holders and politicians who helped her run her government. The ministers serving Jingu also controlled the military.

Before boarding the ships to attack Korea she said, "I will lead our armies into battle. If my plan succeeds all of you will have the credit. If it is a failure I alone shall be to blame."

Then Empress Jingu grasped her battleaxe and commanded the three divisions of her army to "slay not those who lay down their weapons."

From these words and others of equal wisdom the unknown story of Jingu's childhood was built up, layer upon layer, for this book.

People of the Imperial Clan in which Jingu lived as Princess and Empress were far different from the rice farmers and fishermen of the other clans. There were about one hundred clans on the islands of Japan. The commoners were barefoot. They took food from wooden plates with their fingers. Chinese visitors in their writing described the Japanese people as "gentle savages." However, Empress Jingu and her years of leadership were regarded very highly by the Emperor of China and his Court.

Jingu is the most beloved of all Japan's empresses. She was one of the greatest female leaders in the history of the human race.